THOMAS & FRIENDS

™

Contents

Read all about **Thomas** and his **Really Useful** friends!

Say Hello to the Steam Team

Thomas
the blue number 1 Tank Engine
Thomas is a cheeky little engine who always tries to be Really Useful, working hard on his own branch line.

"Bust my buffers! I'm a Really Useful Engine!"

Edward
the blue number 2 Engine
Edward is one of the oldest engines. He's very kind, and when there's trouble, Edward calms things down.

"A steady engine is a Really Useful Engine!"

Henry
the green number 3 Engine
Henry is a long, fast engine. He's very strong, but sometimes he's a bit of a worrier.

"Bubbling boilers!"

Gordon
the blue number 4 Express Engine
Gordon is one of the fastest and strongest engines – and he knows it! He pulls the big Express.

"Fastest and best, I pull the Express!"

James
the red number 5 Engine
James is very proud of his shiny red paint. He can pull passenger coaches as well as freight.

"Mind my paintwork!"

Percy
the green number 6 Engine
Percy is the small engine who delivers all the mail on the Island of Sodor. It keeps him very busy!

"Have to hurry, mail coming through!"

Toby
the brown number 7 Tram Engine
Toby is always happy when he's working hard at the Quarry with his coach, Henrietta.

"Gosh! Fizzling fireboxes!"

Emily
the dark green Engine
Emily is a kind-hearted engine who always helps her friends if they are in trouble.

"Excellent Emily can do it!"

If you were a **Steam Team engine,** which one would you be?

Too Many Wheels

One day Spencer was taking the Duke and Duchess of Boxford to Callan Castle for Lord Callan's birthday ball. They had a special gift for him.

"Now remember, Spencer, I want to arrive in good time," said the Duke.

"Don't worry, sir," said Spencer. "I won't let you down!"

At Knapford Station, The Thin Controller arrived on his bicycle to see The Fat Controller. "You should get a car," said The Fat Controller.

"I prefer my bicycle," said The Thin Controller. "**TWO** wheels are best."

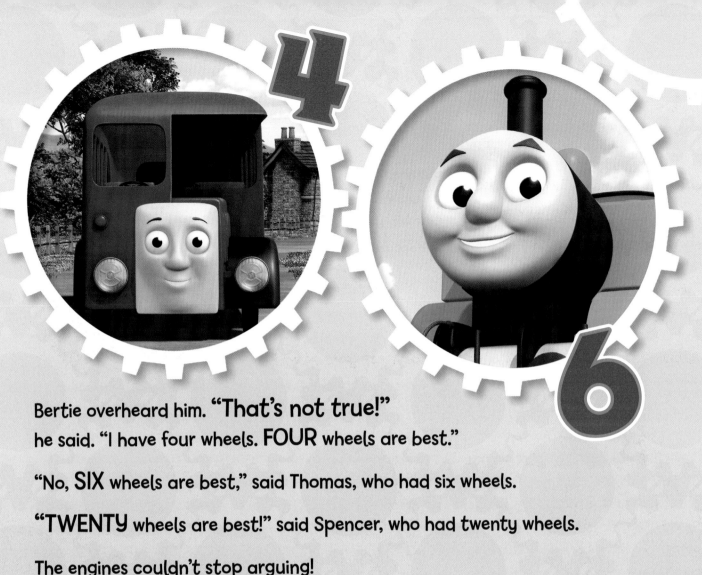

Bertie overheard him. "That's not true!"
he said. "I have four wheels. FOUR wheels are best."

"No, SIX wheels are best," said Thomas, who had six wheels.

"TWENTY wheels are best!" said Spencer, who had twenty wheels.

The engines couldn't stop arguing!
"No, no, no. FOUR wheels!" said Bertie.

"SIX wheels!" said Thomas.

"TWENTY wheels!" said Spencer, and they all puffed away.

Spencer sped along, but there was trouble! There was a loud bang and a **hissssss** of steam. His valve gear had **snapped!**

"Peep! Peep!" said Thomas, stopping beside Spencer. "Have your **TWENTY** wheels let you down? **SIX** wheels to the rescue! I'll take your passengers for you."

hisssssss

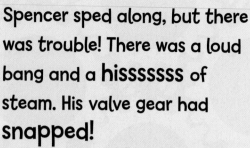

6

Peep! Peep!

Thomas steamed along proudly. But there was more trouble! A tree had fallen across the line. "Oh, no!" cried Thomas, slamming on his brakes. "Phew! That was close."

Toot! Toot! Bertie arrived. "I'll take the Duke by road!" he said. "After all, FOUR wheels are best!"

Bertie sped along, but there was even more trouble when pins on the road burst his tyre: POP!

Bertie swerved, then came to a stop. "Whoaaoh!" he said. "Flat tyre, sir. Sorry."

toot! toot!

4

POP!

Ring, ring! Ring, ring! Along came The Thin Controller on his bicycle. "We need to get to Callan Castle," the Duke told him.

"I'll get help," said The Thin Controller, and he rode off to the phone box to call for help. "TWO wheels to the rescue!" he said.

A few minutes later, Harold the Helicopter arrived!

"Hop on!" said Harold when he landed. "I'll get you to Callan Castle!" And he did just that!

4

6

20

That night, Spencer, Bertie and Thomas chatted about their day. **"Two, four, six, twenty?** I still don't know how many wheels are best," said Thomas. "But it was **Harold** who saved the day ... and he doesn't have **any wheels at all!"**

0

A Jigsaw Picture

Peep! Moo! Thomas stops to let the cows cross the line.
Where do the little jigsaw pieces fit into the picture?

1

2

3

16

Answers are on page 68.

Special Delivery

Thomas is needed at Brendam Docks! Move your finger through the maze to show him the way.

FINISH

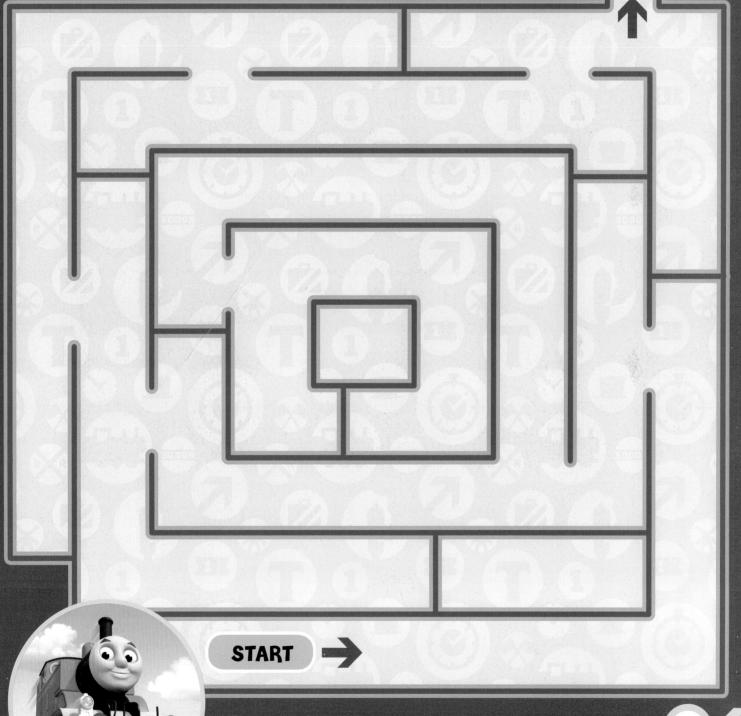

START →

Answers are on page 68.

Inspection Day

It's Inspection Day! The Fat Controller makes sure all the engines are clean and tidy.
Can you see the little close-ups in the big picture?
Tick ✔ a box when you find one.

1

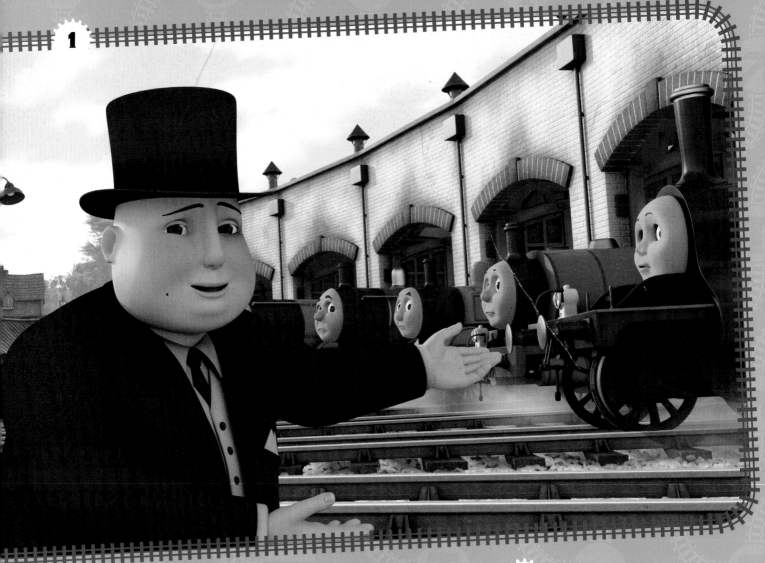

a

b

c

Clever Thomas has found the Inspector's gold watch.
Tick ✔ a box when you find a close-up in the big picture.

2

a  ☑

b  ☑

c  ☑

Say Hello to Stephen

Stephen is a jolly old engine who likes to laugh and joke. The smaller engines go to him for good advice. He works at Ulfstead Castle and he sometimes pulls a blue open-top carriage.

Stephen is ...

golden-yellow and black, with a white funnel.

Stephen has ...

a gold nameplate with ROCKET on it.

Stephen says ...

"They used to call me The Rocket, because I was so speedy!"

Which 2 pictures of Stephen are the same?

Turn the page to read a story about Stephen.

21

Answers are on page 68.

Slow Stephen

Read the story about Stephen. When you see a picture, say the name.

 **Stephen**

 **Gordon**

 **James**

 **Thomas**

You can make **PING**, **PEEP** and **SNAP** noises, too!

 used to be so fast that the other

engines called him The Rocket. But now

is old, and very slow. "You're too slow to be

Really Useful!" said  . "Yes,

 , get out of my way!" said  .

Then  remembered something.

"Did you hear a noise as you crossed the

bridge?"  asked  . "I go

far too fast to hear noises!" said  .

"And I didn't hear anything, ,"

said . Later, was on

the bridge when a bolt fell off - PING -

and the bridge started to shake and

c-r-e-a-k !

 huffed off to warn the others.

"The bridge is damaged!" he told .

"I must stop ! , you

block this side." Just then, "PEEP!

Express coming through!" cried .

 blocked the bridge and cried,

"Stop, , stop!" "Out of

the way!" cried , as he braked,

and stopped just in time.

 was telling  off when

- **SNAP!** - the bridge cables snapped!

 realised what could have

happened. " , you saved me!"

said  . The Fat Controller was

pleased with  and  .

"You were Really Useful Engines today,

and **Really Useful heroes!"**

he said. And  agreed!

Happy Thomas

Use blue, yellow and red to colour in this picture of happy Thomas! The little picture will help you.

Why do you think Thomas is smiling?

Thomas Racing

The Steam Team is very fast!
How fast can you do these things?
Ask a grown-up to time you.

Say your **name** and **address**.

Do **5** star jumps.

Say an engine name that begins with the **t** sound.

Say the name of a **green** engine.

Touch your toes **3** times.

Say Hello to Cranky

Cranky the Crane works at Brendam Docks. He likes to keep an eye on things from high up on his tall tower legs. Sometimes, Cranky can be a bit grumpy!

Cranky is ...

dark green and black.

Cranky has ...

a big hook on the end of his long arm.

Cranky says ...

"There's nothing I can't lift!"

28

Cranky has lots of jobs to do. Join the dots to draw what he's unloading.

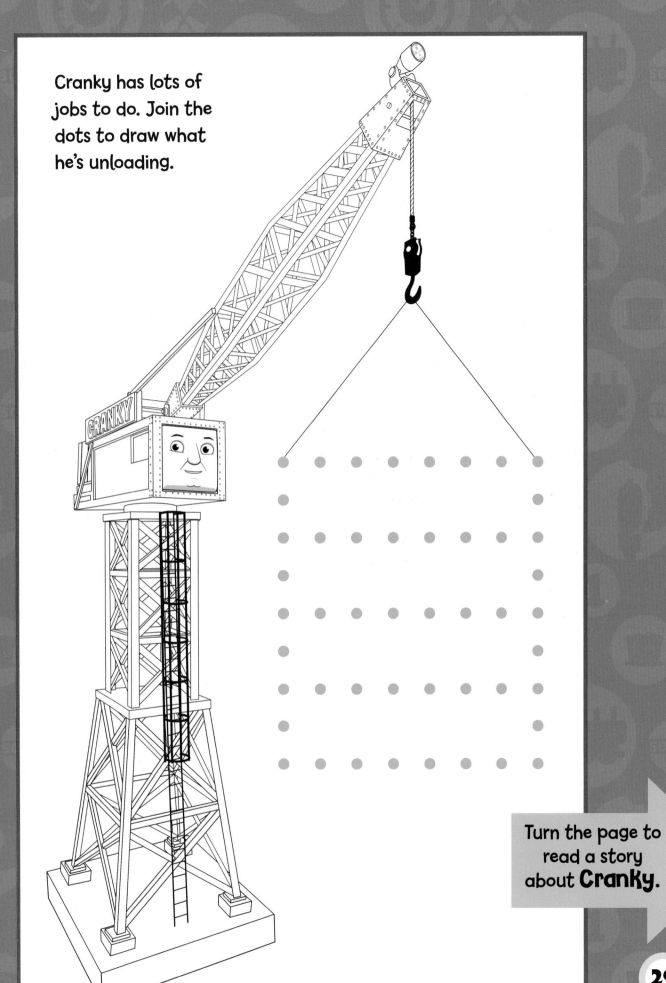

Turn the page to read a story about **Cranky.**

A Cranky Christmas

It was Christmas, and Thomas was busy being Really Useful. But the rails were icy, and his wheels slipped and slid. "Whoaa! Bust my buffers!" he cried.

"Whoaa! Bust my buffers!"

A workman filled Thomas' sandbox with sand. "It's to help you grip the rails," Edward told him.

The Fat Controller asked Thomas to collect a Christmas crate from the Docks and take it to the Town Hall. "It's a special surprise," he explained.

"Oh, no!"

At the Docks, Cranky was unloading the crate when he dropped it, and it landed with a **crash** and a rattle!

"Oh, no, it's broken!" said Cranky, and he hid the crate, and told Thomas he hadn't seen it.

Thomas chuffed off to tell The Fat Controller, but he went so **fast** that his wheels slipped and slid on the icy tracks.

"Whoaa!" he cried, but then he remembered his sandbox, and he emptied sand onto the rails so his wheels could grip.

The Fat Controller and the Mayor were waiting for him. "Cranky doesn't know where the Christmas crate is," Thomas told them. "But don't worry, I'll find it! I'll search the Docks from **top to bottom!**"

Edward watched as Thomas steamed off again. "Thomas, you need to refill your sandbox!" he called. But Thomas didn't hear him ...

At the Docks, Thomas looked everywhere for the Christmas crate. When Salty spotted it at last, Thomas set off with it.

But there was trouble! Near the station Thomas hit an icy patch and slid out of control. And his sandbox was empty! "I can't stop!" he cried. **"HELP!"**

Edward raced to the rescue! He emptied his sandbox on the line just in time. **"Brake, Thomas, brake!"** he cried.

"Nooooo!"

Thomas braked, and screeched to a stop. But - CRASH! - the crate fell onto the platform. "Nooooo!" cried Thomas. "I've broken the Christmas surprise!"

But The Fat Controller wasn't angry. "Don't worry, Thomas!" he said, showing him what was inside: ice skates, and boards to build an **ice rink.** And nothing was broken!

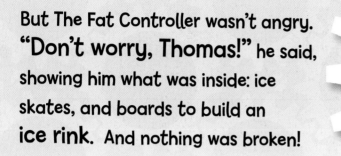

When the ice rink was ready, Thomas and Edward watched everyone skating – even The Fat Controller! "Ice looks **fun** after all," said Thomas. "But now it's The Fat Controller who needs some sand to stop **slipping** and **sliding!**"

That night, Thomas told Salty how glad he was that the ice rink hadn't been broken.

"That's what I was worried about when I dropped it," said Cranky. "It's why I hid it."

"You DROPPED it?" said Thomas, eyes wide. "And HID it?"

Cranky nodded. "I'm sorry," he said. "VERY sorry! But can we forget about it? After all, it is Christmas!"

Salty smiled. "Aye, Cranky's right!" he said. "Let's have a sing-song. I'll start.
We wish you a Merry Christmas, and a Cranky New Year!"

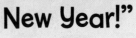

Christmas Fun

At Christmas time there is a tree and lights at every station! Draw lines to match the baubles to the ones on the tree.

How many red lights can you count? Tick ✔ the number.

1 ☐   **2** ☐   **3** ☐

Answers are on page 68.

Bouncing Balls

Boing!
Boing!
Boing!

When Thomas shunts the trucks too hard, a crate breaks open and red balls bounce around! Count the balls in picture 1 and draw a circle round the number.

1   2   3   4   5

1 Boing!

2 Boing!

How many balls can you count in picture 2? Circle the number.

1   2   3   4   5

37

Answers are on page 68.

Who Am I?

Can you match the clues to the engines, and say the names?

Gordon

1
I am green.

I deliver the mail.

My number is 6.

Who am I?

Percy

2
I am very proud of my red paint.

My number is 5.

I am a Really Splendid engine.

Who am I?

3
I am blue.

I pull the Express.

My number is 4.

Who am I?

James

Answers are on page 68.

Ashima

Flying Scotsman

Gordon

Thomas

Let's Race!

Say Hello to Spencer

Spencer is a shiny express engine. He's very fast, and is owned by a Duke and Duchess. He thinks his work is very important, and he doesn't like doing ordinary jobs like shunting.

Spencer is ...

super shiny silver!

Spencer calls himself ...

Spencer the Grand.

Spencer says ...

"I'm shining and gleaming and ready to steam!"

What do you know about Spencer? Tick ✔ the true fact and cross ✘ the false fact.

a Spencer is red.　　✔　✘

b Spencer is fast.　　✔　✘

Turn the page to read a story about **Spencer**.

41

Answers are on page 68.

Story: The Beast of Sodor

Read the story about Spencer and Henry.
When you see a picture, say the name.

Spencer

Henry

Emily

The Fat Controller

You can make **SCREECH**, **HISS** and **PEEP** noises, too!

One snowy day,  sent  to

work with  .  started

showing off. "Once I saved the Duke from

the **Abominable Snowman**, a scary

snow beast!" told  .

That scared poor  !

 and  were chuffing

along when they saw a tall spray of snow

and  braked, SCREECH!

"It's the Abominable Snowman!"

said  , and  shivered.

The snow came closer, then ... "Hello,

 ," said a voice. It was  ,

who was ploughing snow off the rails.

"Oh, what a relief, it's only you,  ,"

said  .

Later, when a big, snowy figure walked

towards and , it was

 who was scared! "AARGH!"

said , as his valve burst, HISS!

"Don't leave me, !" cried .

 was scared, but – PEEP! – blew

his whistle so loudly that the snow beast

jumped, and the snow fell off. It was

, who was lost in the snow!

 was proud of  . "You

are a brave and Really Useful Engine,

 ," said  . "You helped

 even when you thought I was

the **Abominable Snowman!"**

was still so scared that his eyes were

closed. "  , is that you? Has it gone?"

 whispered.  winked, and

 just smiled!

Really Useful Engines

The Fat Controller always has important jobs for Thomas, Percy, James and Gordon to do. They all love being **Really Useful** Engines!

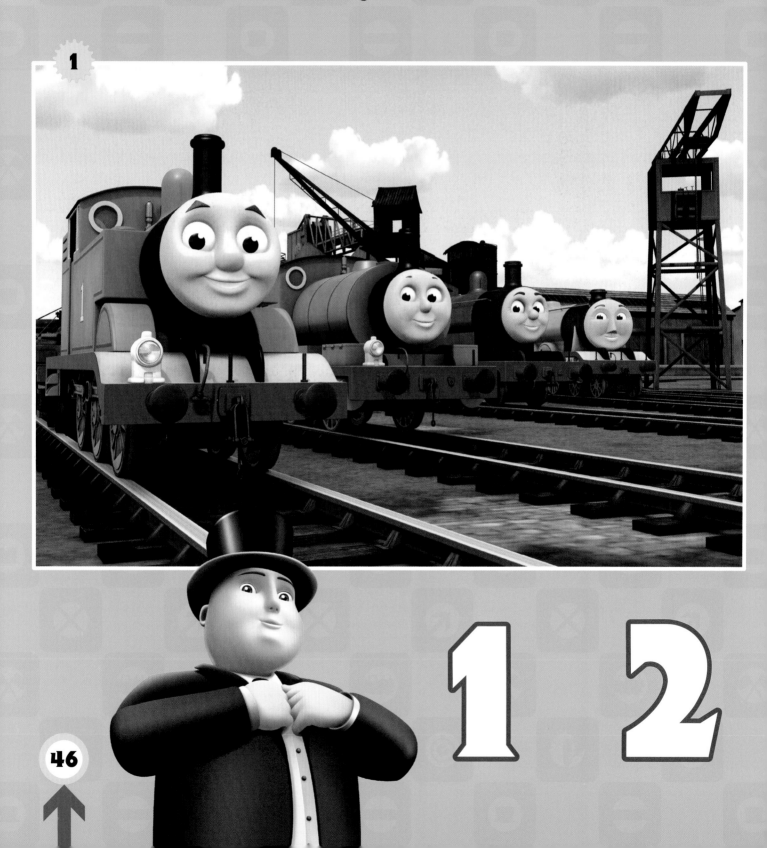

1

2

These pictures look the same, but there are 5 differences in picture 2.
Can you spot them all and colour in a number for each difference you find?

3 4 5

Answers are on page 68.

Ready, Steady, Go!

Fizzling fireboxes!
Thomas and Percy love
having a race!
Play the game
with a friend to
see who wins.

HOW TO PLAY

★ Place a counter or button each
on START.
★ On your turn, flip a coin. If it
lands **heads** up, move 1 space
along the track. If it lands
tails up move 2 spaces.
★ When you land on a **green**
space, have an extra turn.
★ When you land on a **red** space,
go back 1 space.
★ The first one to reach FINISH
is the winner.

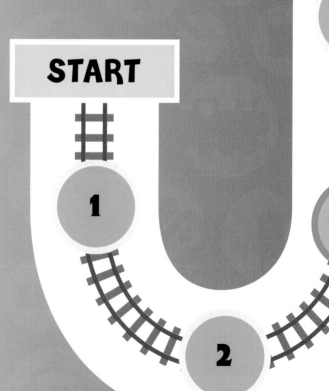

START

1
2
3
4
5
6

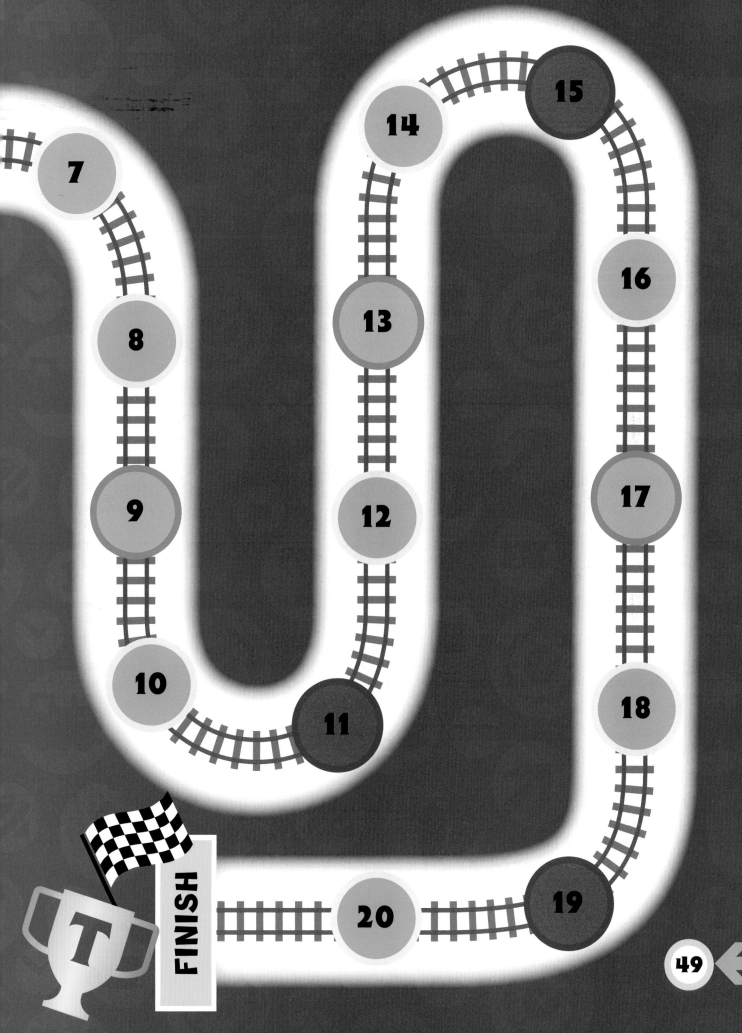

Poor Henry is a bit of a worrier! When he saw the red chicken pox spots on The Fat Controller's grandchildren's faces, he was VERY worried.

"Oooooo, SPOTS!" said Henry. "What if engines can catch chicken pox?"

"Oooooo, SPOTS!"

Thomas was at the farm collecting chickens when Butch the breakdown truck got stuck in the mud. His engine revved and his big wheels spun – and Thomas got covered in mud!

"You're all spotty!" laughed Butch.

Thomas laughed too. "Don't worry, Butch," he said. "It's only a bit of mud!"

"It's only a bit of mud!"

When Henry saw Thomas' spots, he was very worried. **"Ugh!"** he cried. **"Spots!** And chickens! I knew it! Engines **DO** get chicken pox!"

That afternoon, the station was being repainted when there was a little accident with a tin of paint. It was **RED** paint, and spots of it ended up on Gordon's face.

When Henry saw Gordon's spots, he was in such a panic that he set off **BACKWARDS!**
"Chicken pox!" he cried. **"Gordon, get away!"**

"Some engines ..." groaned Gordon.

"Gordon, get away!"

The Fat Controller was surprised to see Henry going backwards! "What are you doing?" he called.

But Henry just rushed on until he finally came to a stop at Wellsworth Station, and Thomas pulled up in front of him.

Henry saw that Thomas didn't have spots anymore.

"Thomas?" said Henry. "Is that you? Where are your spots? Your chicken pox spots?"

"Spots?" said Thomas. "They weren't spots. I just had mud on my face. I've been to the Washdown to get it washed off."

Gordon overheard. "And these aren't chicken pox spots on my face," he said. "I just got covered in red paint!"

"Mud? Paint? But I thought you both had chicken pox!" said Henry.

"Mud?"

"Paint?"

Thomas laughed. "Chicken pox? Steamies don't get chicken pox!" he said.

"No, even **chickens** don't get chicken pox!" added Gordon.

"Yes, only **people** get chicken pox," The Fat Controller explained.

After that, Henry stopped worrying about chicken pox spots and got back to work. He was glad to be a **Really Useful** Engine again, and not a **Really Worried** one!

"Yes, only people get chicken pox!"

Snowmen!

When it snows, the engines say hello to the snowmen by the tracks!

1 Which snowman is the biggest?

2 Which snowman has only 1 stick arm?

3 Which snowman is the smallest?

56

Answers are on page 68.

STEAM TEAM GO

BEST

FRIENDS

Say Hello to Hiro

Hiro lived on a railway in Japan before he came to the Island of Sodor many years ago. He was so sleek and fast that everyone called him Master of the Railway.

Hiro is ...

black and gold.

Hiro's number is ...

51

Hiro says ...

"I made lots of new friends when I came to the Island of Sodor."

Colour in the 4 letters in the name HIRO.

HGITRLO

Turn the page to read a story about **Hiro**.

Answers are on page 68.

Helping Hiro

One day, Thomas was waiting for his load of pipes to be strapped down when he met his friend Hiro.

They steamed off together, but Thomas set off before the pipes were loaded properly, and there was trouble!

Near a bend, Thomas pulled ahead of Hiro. "I'm faster than you!" he peeped.

"Slow down!" cried Hiro.

"Slow down!"

"Whooooaaaa!"

"Whooooaaaa!" cried Thomas,
and he braked so hard that the pipes
fell on to the line in front of Hiro!

Hiro braked, too, but his wheels
ran off the track! "Oooohhh!"
he groaned.

"Oooohhh!"

Rocky took Hiro to the Steamworks for repairs, and
that night, Thomas told Percy about the accident.

"It was all my fault," he said. "Hiro is from far away,
and it's not easy to get the spare parts he needs!"

The next day, Thomas set off to look for spare parts in the wood where Hiro had broken down before. But the wood was **dark,** and a bit **scary** ...

PEEEP!

When a deer ran in front of Thomas he slammed on his brakes, but the rails gave way and he ended up in the mud. Thomas was stuck!

"PEEEP!" called Thomas. "HELP! HELP!" But no one heard him ...

"HELP! HELP!"

Huff! Puff!

Then Thomas had an idea. **Huff! Puff!** He **huffed** and **puffed** and **blew** steam out of his funnel – and Harold the Helicopter saw it! "That's **steam** from an engine!" he said.

Then, "PEEP, PEEEEP!" peeped Thomas.

"And that's **Thomas!**" said Harold, and he flew off to get help.

"That's Thomas!"

Soon it got **very dark**, and the rails shook. "What's that?" whispered Thomas, but it was only Percy, Rocky – and The Fat Controller.

"I ... I was trying to help Hiro, sir," said Thomas. "I was looking for ..."

Suddenly a deer leapt out, and everyone jumped: "Whaaa!" Then they all **laughed** when they saw that it was only a deer.

"**Whaaa!**"

When Thomas was fixed, he went to find Hiro. "I wish you were repaired, too," said Thomas.

"But I am!" laughed Hiro. "The Fat Controller got lots of parts for me. I'm as good as new."

"Peeeeep!" peeped Thomas happily, and the two friends whizzed off happily together!

The Fat Controller's Quiz

Can you answer these questions about Thomas and his friends?

2

Whose shadow is this?

1

Where does Cranky work?

☑ Brendam Docks

☑ the Quarry

3

Thomas is a red express engine.

☑ true

☑ false

4

Where did Hiro live before he came to the Island of Sodor?

☑ Japan

☑ America

5

Join the dots to write Percy's number.

6

6

Who is this engine?

Well done! You are Really Clever!
The medal is for you!
Colour it in, and write your name on the line.

....

won this medal.

Answers

Page 16 A Jigsaw Picture

Page 17 Special Delivery

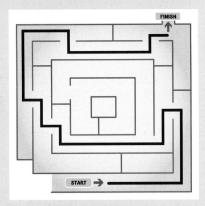

Page 18 Inspection Day

Page 21 Say Hello to Stephen

Pictures b and c are the same.

Page 36 Christmas Fun

There are 3 red lights.

Page 37 Bouncing Balls

1 - 2 balls, 2 - 4 balls.

Page 38 Who Am I?

1 - Percy, 2 - James, 3 - Gordon.

Page 41 Say Hello to Spencer

a - false, b - true.

Page 46 Really Useful Engines

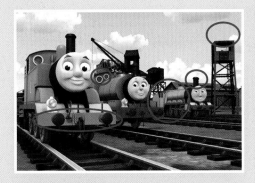

Page 56 Snowmen!

1 - c, 2 - f, 3 - d.

Page 59 Say Hello to Hiro

HIRO

Page 66 The Fat Controller's Quiz

1 - Brendam Docks, 2 - Toby, 3 - false, 4 - Japan, 5 - 6, 6 - Emily.